Last Night I Saw a Dream

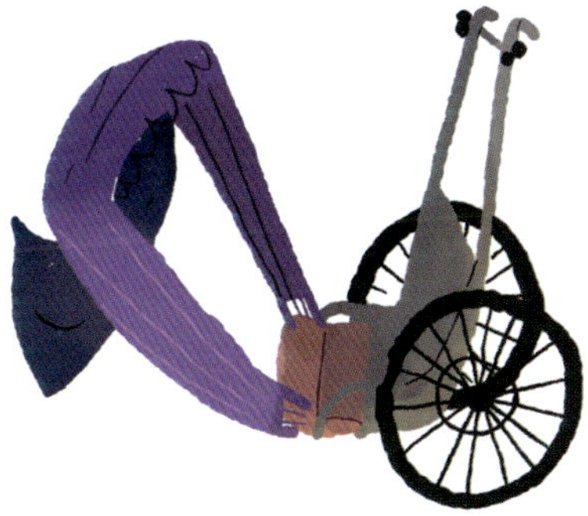

TALKING CUB
Published by Speaking Tiger Books LLP
125A, Ground Floor, Shahpur Jat
New Delhi 110049

First published in paperback in Talking Cub by Speaking Tiger Books in 2021

ISBN: 978-93-5447-100-1
eISBN: 978-93-5447-101-8

10 9 8 7 6 5 4 3 2 1

Printed at PRINTWORKS, New Delhi, India

Last Night I Saw a Dream

Written by

Rabindranath Tagore

Illustrated by

Adrija Ghosh

Translated by

Sudeshna Shome Ghosh

talking CUB

An Imprint of Speaking Tiger Books

Last night I was all dreamy
'Look!' said little Binu
as she shook me.

And I heard, what a clanging and knocking–
Kolkata was walking, swinging and dancing!

The brick houses, straight as rhinos,
Were leaping with their doors and windows.

The roads all slithering, like cobra snakes
Carrying trams on their backs, that fell with great shakes.

Shops and markets went up and down,
Roofs banged against roofs and fell all around.

The bells kept tolling

INDIA POST
বর্ণপরিচয়

Our school was running at top speed too:
There went our math, and there our grammar books flew;

The maps on the walls thrashed around
Like birds flapping their wings aloud.

The Howrah bridge was like a giant scorpion,
Walking just beyond was the road Harrison.

The Monument tower swayed like a mad elephant,
Raising its trunk, it trumpeted, loud and inelegant.

However late it was, they rang past noon.
Lakhs and lakhs pleaded, 'Oh stop, stop,
Where will you go? This madness please drop.'

Kolkata listened not, it kept moving
The dancing bug was in every door and hinge.

But I thought to myself, this is fine:
Let Kolkata go straight to Bombay,
Let it go to Dilli, Lahore or Agra,
Then I can wear a turban, and on my feet, nagras.

Or what if it runs straight to Britain?
Then we will be suited and booted, like Englishmen.

Just then, at some sound
my eyes suddenly opened,

I saw Kolkata was in Kolkata,
and I had awoken.

Rabindranath Tagore (1861-1941) was a poet, writer as well as a musician. He wrote over 2,000 songs, numerous short stories, novels, plays, essays, poetry and dance dramas. Among his songs are the national anthems of two countries—India and Bangladesh. Tagore was awarded the Nobel Prize for Literature in 1913.

Adrija is from Calcutta, lives in Bangalore and works as an illustrator. She can never have too many notebooks and too much chocolate cake.

Sudeshna spends her day among books, editing, reading, writing or stacking them on the shelves of her library.